Little Brown Child

by
Lara Washington

Illustrations by MikeMotz.com

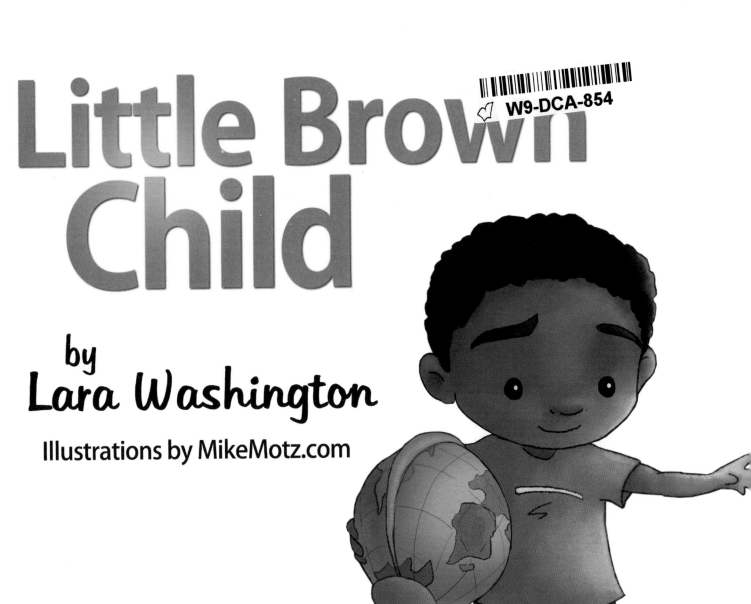

This book is dedicated
to my son Christopher Paul Dunn
who inspired me to write this poem.

Little Brown Child

ISBN-13: 978-1484035801
ISBN: 1484035801

Printed in the U.S.A.

Little Brown Child

by
Lara Washington

Illustrations by MikeMotz.com

Little brown child,
If you look into my eyes,
Little brown child,
I can tell you who you are.
You are beauty, you are pride,
There is nothing you should hide.

Little brown child,
There is something you should know.
Little brown child,
When you are feeling sad and low,
Open up your eyes and see
It is you who holds the key.

Little brown child,
Happiness starts with a smile.
Little brown child,
Laugh or giggle for a while.
You will see and hear the joys
Echoed out by girls and boys.

Little brown child,
Sometimes life is so unkind.
Little brown child,
Let no one steal your peace of mind.
Stand up on your feet and go.
This is how you learn to grow.

Little brown child,
Never hide behind a mask.
Little brown child,
If you want to know, just ask.
Understanding history
leads the way to victory.

Little brown child,
Every time you help a friend,
Little brown child,
Good comes back around again.
Keep on reaching out to share;
It will show how much you care.

Little brown child,
When you're scared, it's okay.
Little brown child,
Your strength will guide you day by day.
Listen to the words I say:
You will always find a way.

Little brown child,
Do your very best in school.
Little brown child,
Always listen to this rule:
If you feed your brain with knowledge,
It will steer you straight to college.

Little brown child,
Water falls outside your eyes.
Little brown child,
To lend a hand at painful times.
Hold your face up to the sky,
And those tears will slowly dry.

Little brown child,
Explore around the world you live.
Little brown child,
And keep the things you learn active.
With great curiosity,
You'll flow like electricity.

Little brown child,
When your spirit feels alone,
Little brown child,
And you really want to moan,
You must stand upon your throne
And conquer the great unknown.

Little brown child,
By and by you will be challenged.
Little brown child,
The universe keeps things in balance.
Face hard tasks with lots of courage;
It will help you through your voyage.

Little brown child,
Come and see the shining stars.
Little brown child,
Can you tell me who they are?

We
are
beauty,
we
are
pride.
There
is
nothing
we
should
hide!